Tacky's Christmas

To the best Christmas gifts I've ever had:
Robin, Rob & Jodi, Jamie & Danyle, Kate, Andrew
—and those to come.
Thanks, H

For Penny's grandsons, Lionel and Tiernan.
—L

Houghton Mifflin Books for Children is an imprint of
Houghton Mifflin Harcourt Publishing Company.

www.hmhbooks.com

The text of this book is set in Garamond.

Library of Congress Cataloging-in-Publication Data is on file.

ISBN 978-0-547-17208-8

Manufactured in China
LEO 10 9 8 7 6 5 4 3 2 1
4500220109

Tacky's Christmas

Written by Helen Lester
Illustrated by Lynn Munsinger

Houghton Mifflin Books for Children
Houghton Mifflin Harcourt
BOSTON NEW YORK 2010

Christmas had come to Nice Icy Land.

Excitement was in the air.

And in the water.

And in the ice cubes.

Goodly, Lovely, Angel, Neatly, and Perfect had everything beautifully organized.

"First we must wrap our presents," they said.

But wait. Where was Tacky?

Where Tacky *was* was in the chimney.

Practicing.

And stuck.

He had been selected to wear the Santa outfit since his belly shook like a bowl full of jelly when he laughed.

Eventually his companions found him, and
with much huffing and oofing

—*phwwop*—

they pulled him out.

Present wrapping was very secret, so each penguin hid behind
a block of ice.

Shh . . .

Now that the presents were wrapped, it was time to turn to the task of making ornaments. As they worked with glue and glitter and sequins, the penguins sang their favorite carol:

Deck the iceberg, wrap a gifty
Fa la la la la la la la la
Make an ornament that's nifty
Fa la la la la la la la la
Hang it on a tree—

A tree?
The penguins looked around.

There seemed to be a shortage of trees
in Nice Icy Land.

"We could decorate Tacky," suggested Goodly and Lovely.

"He's sort of tree-shaped, if a bit heavy on the lower part,"
added Angel, Neatly, and Perfect.
"Hey, suit me up!" cried Tacky.

And so they did.

It was a red tree and they'd been dreaming of
a green Christmas, but never mind.

With the presents under the Tackytree,
there was only one thing left to do.

Open the gifts!

Goodly gave each penguin a jar of belly-sliding slickum.

Lovely offered zippy speed flippers.

Angel's gift was snappy bow ties.

Neatly provided feather dusters so they could dust their feathers.

Perfect gave bottles of Yellow Brand Beak and Foot Polish.

Finally, Tacky presented each of his companions with

A CAN OF SHAVING CREAM.

Shaving cream? For penguins?
Goodly, Lovely, Angel, Neatly, and Perfect were speechless.
So Tacky took over.
"Hey, this is really fun stuff. Let me show you."
And then squirt . . .
Goodly, Lovely, Angel, Neatly, and Perfect were about to duck
when suddenly they were interrupted by the *thump* . . .
thump . . . *thump* of feet in the distance.

"Oh, no!" they cried. "It's the hunters. On Christmas yet!"
But Tacky was in full squirt mode.
He zapped Goodly and Lovely, who pleaded, "Tacky, the hunters are coming!"
"This is so cool!" *Squirt*. Angel got it next.

And meanwhile, the hunters were approaching with rocks and locks and maps and traps, and they were rough and tough.

As the *thump . . . thump . . . thump* drew closer, the penguins could hear their growly voices chanting,

We're gonna march some pretty penguins
And we'll drag 'em through the snow
And we'll take away their Christmas giftzies
HO. HO. HO.

"Puh-lease, Tacky!" begged his companions.
But Tacky was having too much fun.
He squirted Neatly and Perfect.
"Here ya go!"
It takes a lot to make a penguin shiver, but by now
Goodly, Lovely, Angel, Neatly, and Perfect were
crouching behind Tacky. Shivering.
The hunters drew closer and closer, and finally they
thumped right up to Tacky.

Stopped.

Then stared.

And then, most surprising, they broke into big silly grins.

"Whoa! Him's not a pretty penguin. Him's
Sandy Clawz! Looky that beardy! And him's
got jewels and sequins and sprinkles.
Gotta be Sandy Clawz!"

Shyly, respectfully, adoringly, the hunters bowed.

Goodly, Lovely, Angel, Neatly, and Perfect peeked out
from behind Tacky. The hunters gasped.

"Why, looky, them's Sandy's elfies! Them's got
beardzes too. Whoa, looky that!
Merry Christmas, elfies!"

"Merry Christmas," the penguins
bubbled back.

Well, of course, there was only one thing to do.

After all, it was Christmas. A special time of giving and sharing.

So the penguins invited the hunters to stay and enjoy their fish pudding.

Tacky came down the chimney.

Before dinner.

They sang and played games and told jokes,
and everyone was filled with the Christmas
spirit and had the merriest Christmas ever.

And much, much later, after the happy hunters had departed,
Goodly, Lovely, Angel, Neatly, and Perfect hugged Tacky.
Tacky was an odd bird, but a nice bird to have around
—especially at Christmas.